STORIES ABOUT
GIANTS, WITCHES
AND DRAGONS
TO READ ALOUD

Compiled by OSCAR WEIGLE

Illustrated by SERGIO LEONE

WONDER BOOKS • NEW YORK

CONTENTS

Note to Parents

One of the most gratifying ways of bringing the precious feeling of closeness to your family is sharing the joys of reading with your children. More and more parents are discovering the pleasures of a daily Storytime Hour . . . a time for reading aloud to young children, helping them develop a lifetime love of books, stimulating their imagination, enriching their vocabularies, and teaching them fascinating facts about the world around them.

Read-Aloud books are especially planned for the small child who loves to listen to a story— and also for the beginning reader who is proud of his new talent and wants to show it off for your approval.

You will enjoy reading these stories to your young children. You will enjoy them perhaps even more when your child proudly reads the stories to you.

THE GIANTS AND THE HERD-BOY

THERE was once upon a time a poor boy who had neither father nor mother. In order to gain a living he looked after the sheep of a great lord. Day and night he spent out in the open fields, and only when it was very wet and stormy did he take refuge in a little hut on the edge of a big forest.

One night, when he was sitting beside his flocks, he heard the sound of someone crying. He got up and followed the direction of the noise. To his astonishment he found a giant lying at the entrance of the wood.

He was about to run off when the giant called out: "Don't be afraid—I won't harm you. On the contrary, I will reward you if you will bind up my foot. I hurt it when I was trying to root up an oak tree." The herd-boy took off his shirt and bound the giant's wounded foot with it.

Then the giant got up and said: "Now I will reward you. We are going to celebrate a marriage today, and I promise you we shall have plenty of fun. Come and enjoy yourself, but in order that my brothers may not see you, put this band round your waist and then you'll be invisible."

With these words he handed the herd-boy a belt, and walking on in front, he led him to a fountain, where hundreds of giants and giantesses were assembled preparing to hold a wedding.

They danced and played different games till midnight. Then one of the giants tore up a plant by its roots, and all the giants and giantesses made themselves so thin that they disappeared into the earth through the hole made by the uprooting of the plant. The wounded giant remained behind to the last and called out: "Herd-boy, where are you?"

"Here I am, close to you," was the reply.

"Touch me," said the giant, "so that you, too, may come with us."

The herd-boy did as he was told, and before he would have believed it possible, he found himself in a big hall, where the walls were made of pure gold. Then to his astonishment he saw that the hall was furnished with the tables and chairs that belonged to his master.

In a few minutes the company began to eat and drink, and when the youth had eaten and drunk as much as he could, he thought to himself, "Why shouldn't I put a loaf of bread in my pocket? I shall be glad of it tomorrow." So he seized a loaf and put it under his tunic.

No sooner had he done so than the wounded giant limped up to him and whispered softly: "Herd-boy, where are you?"

"Here I am," replied the youth.

"Then hold on to me," said the giant, "so that I may lead you up again."

So the herd-boy held on to the giant, and in a few minutes he found himself on the earth once more, but the giant had vanished. The herd-boy returned to his sheep and took off the invisible belt, which he hid carefully in his bag.

The next morning the lad felt hungry and thought he would cut off a piece of the loaf he had carried away from the feast and eat it. But although he tried with all his might, he couldn't cut off the smallest piece! In despair he bit the loaf, and what was his astonishment when a piece of gold fell out of his mouth and rolled at his feet! He bit the bread a second and third time, and each time a piece of gold fell out of his mouth, but the bread remained untouched.

The herd-boy was delighted over his good fortune, and hiding the magic loaf in his bag, he hurried off to the nearest village to buy himself something to eat. Then he returned to his sheep.

Now, the lord whose sheep the herd-boy looked after had a very lovely daughter who always smiled and nodded to the youth when she walked with her father in his fields. For a long time the herd-boy had made up his mind to prepare a surprise for her on her birthday. So when the day approached, he put on his invisible belt, took a sack of gold pieces with him, and slipping into her room in the middle of the night, he placed the bag of gold beside her bed and returned to his sheep.

The girl's joy was great, and so was her parents' next day when they found the sackful of gold pieces. The herd-boy was so pleased to think of the pleasure he had given that the next night he placed another bag of gold beside the girl's bed.

This he continued to do for seven nights, and the girl and her parents made up their minds that it must be a good fairy who brought the gold every night. But one night they determined to watch and see from their hiding-place who the bringer of the sack of gold really was.

On the eighth night a storm of wind and rain came on while the herd-boy was on his way to bring the beautiful girl another bag of gold. Then for the first time he noticed, just as he reached his master's house, that he had forgotten the belt which made him invisible. He didn't like the idea of going back to his hut in the wind and wet, so he just stepped as he was into the girl's room, laid the sack of gold beside her, and was turning to leave the room, when his master confronted him and said: "You young rogue! So you were going to steal the gold that a good fairy brings every night, were you?"

The herd-boy was so taken aback by his words that he stood trembling before him and did not dare to explain his presence.

Then his master spoke: "As you have always behaved well in my service, I will not send you to prison; but go at once and never let me see your face again."

So the herd-boy went back to his hut, and taking his loaf and belt with him, he went to the nearest town. There he bought himself some fine clothes and a beautiful coach with four horses, hired two servants, and drove back to his master.

Imagine how astonished he was to see his herd-boy returning to him in this manner!

Then the youth told him of the piece of good luck that had befallen him and asked him for the hand of his beautiful daughter. This was readily granted, and the two lived in peace and happiness ever after.

11

PINKEL AND THE WITCH

L ONG, long ago there lived a widow who had three sons. The two eldest were grown up, and though they were known to be lazy, some of the neighbors had given them work to do because of the respect in which their mother was held. But at the time this story begins they had both been so careless and idle that their masters declared they would keep them no longer.

So home they went to their mother and youngest brother, of whom they thought little, because he made himself useful about the house, looked after the hens, and milked the cow. "Pinkel," they called him in scorn, and thereafter "Pinkel" became his name throughout the village.

The two young men thought it was much nicer to live at home and be idle than to do work they did not like, and they would have stayed by the fire till the end of their lives had not the widow lost patience with them and said that since they would not look for work at home, they must seek it elsewhere, for she would not have them under her roof any longer.

But she repented bitterly of her words when Pinkel told her that he, too, was old enough to go out into the world, and that when he had made a fortune, he would send for his mother to keep house for him.

The widow wept many tears at parting from her youngest son, but since she saw his heart was set upon going with his brothers, she did not try to keep him. So the young men started off cheerfully one morning, never doubting that work such as they might be

13

willing to do would be had for the asking, as soon as their money was spent.

But a few days of wandering opened their eyes. Nobody seemed to want them or, if they did, the young men declared that they were not able to undertake all that the farmers or millers or woodcutters required. The youngest brother, who was wiser, would gladly have done some of the work that the others refused, but he was small and slight and no one thought of offering him any.

Therefore, they went from one place to another, living only on the fruit and nuts they could find in the woods, and getting hungrier every day.

One night, after they had been walking for many hours and were very tired, they came to a large lake with an island in the middle of it. From the island streamed a strong light, by which they could see a boat lying half-hidden in the tall grass.

"Let us take it and row over to the island, where there must be a house," said the eldest brother. "Perhaps they will give us food and shelter." They all got in the boat and rowed across.

As they drew near the island, they saw

that the light came from a golden lantern hanging over the door of a hut, while sweet tinkling music came from some bells attached to the golden horns of a goat which was feeding near the cottage.

The young men's hearts rejoiced as they thought that at last they would be able to rest their weary limbs, and they entered the hut. But they were amazed to see an ugly old woman inside, wrapped in a cloak of gold, which lighted up the whole house. They looked at each other uneasily as she came forward with her daughter, for they knew by the cloak that this was a famous witch.

"What do you want?" she asked, at the same time signaling to her daughter to stir the large pot on the fire.

"We are tired and hungry and need shelter for the night," answered the eldest brother.

"You cannot get it here," said the witch, "but you will find both food and shelter in the palace on the other side of the lake. Take your boat and go, but leave this boy with me —I can find work for him, though something tells me he is quick and clever and will do me ill."

"What harm can a poor boy like me do?" answered Pinkel. "Let me go with my brothers, please."

At last the witch let him go, and he followed his brothers to the boat.

The way was farther than they thought,

and it was morning before they reached the palace.

Now, at last, their luck seemed to have turned, for while the two eldest were given places in the king's stables, Pinkel was taken as page to the little prince. He was a clever and amusing boy, who saw everything that passed under his eyes. The king noticed this, and often used him in his own service, which made his brothers jealous.

Things went on in this way for some time, and every day Pinkel rose in the royal favor. At last the envy of his brothers became so great they could bear it no longer and talked together how best they might ruin his standing with the king. They did not wish to kill him—though, perhaps, they would not have been sorry if they had heard he was dead—but merely wished to remind him that he was after all only a child, not half so old and wise as they.

Their opportunity soon came. It happened to be the king's custom to visit his stables once a week to see if his horses were being properly cared for. The next time he entered the stables, the two brothers managed to be in the way, and when the king praised the

beautiful satin skins of the horses under
their charge and remarked how different
was their condition when his grooms had
first come across the lake, the young men at
once began to speak of the wonderful light
which sprang from the lantern over the hut.
The king, who collected all the rarest things
he could find, inquired at once where he
could get this marvelous lantern.

"Send Pinkel for it, Sire," they said. "It be-
longs to an old witch, who no doubt came by
it in some evil way. But Pinkel has a smooth
tongue and he can get the better of any
woman, old or young."

"Then bid him go this very night!" cried the king. "If he brings me the lantern, I will make him one of the chief men about my person."

Pinkel was much pleased at the thought of his adventure and, without more ado, he borrowed a little boat which lay moored to the shore and rowed over to the island at once. It was late by the time he arrived and almost dark, but he knew by the savory smell that the witch was cooking her supper. So he climbed softly onto the roof and, peering down, watched till the old woman's back was turned, when he quickly took a handful of salt from his pocket and threw it into the pot.

Scarcely had he done this when the witch called her daughter and ordered her to lift the pot off the fire and put the stew into a dish, as it had been cooking quite long enough and she was hungry. But no sooner had she tasted it than she put her spoon down and declared that her daughter must have been meddling with it, for it was impossible to eat anything that was all made of salt.

"Go down to the spring in the valley and

get some fresh water that I may prepare a fresh supper," she cried, "for I feel half-starved."

"But, Mother," answered the girl, "how can I find the well in this darkness? The lantern's rays shed no light down there."

"Well, then, take the lantern with you," answered the witch, "for I must have supper, and there is no water that is nearer."

So the girl took her pail in one hand and the golden lantern in the other, and hastened away to the well, followed by Pinkel, who took care to keep out of the way of the rays of light. When at last she stooped to fill her pail at the well, Pinkel, snatching up the lantern, hurried back to his boat and rowed off from the shore.

He was already a long distance from the island when the witch, who wondered what had become of her daughter, went to the door to look for her. Close around the hut was thick darkness, but what was that bobbing light that streamed across the water? The witch's heart sank as it flashed upon her what had happened.

"Is that you, Pinkel?" cried she.

The youth answered, "Yes, it is I!"

"And are you not a knave for robbing me?" said she.

"Truly, I am," replied Pinkel, rowing faster than ever, for he was afraid that the witch might come after him.

But she had no power on the water, and turned angrily into the hut, muttering to herself all the while:

"Take care! Take care! A second time you will not escape so easily!"

The sun had not yet risen when Pinkel returned to the palace. Entering the king's chamber, he held up the lantern so that its rays might fall upon the bed. In an instant the king awoke and, seeing the golden lantern shedding its light upon him, sprang up and embraced Pinkel with joy.

"Oh, clever one," he cried, "what treasure you have brought me!" Then calling for his attendants, he ordered that rooms be prepared for Pinkel and that the youth might enter his presence at any hour. Besides this, he was to have a seat on the council.

All this made the brothers more envious than before, and they thought again how best they might destroy him. At last they remembered the goat with the golden horns and the bells, and they rejoiced. "For," said they, "this time the old woman will be on the watch, and let him be as clever as he likes, the bells on the horns are sure to warn her."

So when, as before, the king come down to the stables and praised the cleverness of their brother, the young men told him of that other marvel possessed by the witch, the goat with the golden horns.

From this moment the king never closed his eyes at night for longing to possess this wonderful creature. He understood something of the danger there might be in trying to take it, now that the witch's suspicions were aroused, and he spent hours in making plans for outwitting her. But somehow he never could think of anything that would do, and at last, as the brothers had foreseen, he sent for Pinkel.

"I hear," he said, "that the old witch on the island has a goat with golden horns, from which hang bells that tinkle the sweetest music. That goat I must have! But, tell me, how am I to get it? I would give the third part of my kingdom to anyone who would bring it to me."

"I will fetch it myself," answered Pinkel.

This time it was easier for Pinkel to approach the island unseen, as there was no golden lantern to throw its beams over the water. But, on the other hand, the goat slept inside the hut and would therefore have to be taken from under the very eyes of the old woman. How was he to do it? All the way across the lake Pinkel thought and thought, till a plan came into his head which seemed

as if it might do, though he knew it would be very difficult to carry out.

The first thing he did when he reached the shore was to look about for a piece of wood. When he had found it, he hid himself close to the hut till it grew dark, when the witch and her daughter went to bed. Then he crept up and fixed the wood under the door, which opened outward, in such a manner that the more one tried to shut it the more firmly it stuck. And this was what happened when the girl went as usual to bolt the door for the night.

"What are you doing?" asked the witch, as her daughter kept tugging at the handle.

"There is something the matter with the door—it won't shut," she answered.

"Well, leave it alone. There is nobody to hurt us," said the witch, who was very sleepy. And the girl did as she was told and went to bed.

Very soon they both were heard snoring, and Pinkel knew that his time was come. Slipping off his shoes, he stole into the hut on tiptoe, and taking from his pockets some food of which the goat was particularly fond, he laid it under his nose. Then, while the animal was eating it, he stuffed each golden bell with wool which he had also brought with him, stopping every minute to listen, lest the witch would awaken, and he would find himself changed into a dreadful bird or beast. But the snoring still continued, and he went on with his work.

When the last bell was muffled, he took another handful of food out of his pocket and held it out to the goat, which instantly rose to its feet and followed Pinkel, who backed slowly to the door. Once outside, he seized the goat and ran down to his boat.

As soon as he had reached the middle of the lake, Pinkel took the wool out of the bells, which began to tinkle loudly. Their sound awoke the witch, who cried out:

"Is that you, Pinkel?"

"Yes, it is I," said Pinkel.

"Have you stolen my golden goat?"

"Yes, I have," answered Pinkel.

"Are you not a knave, Pinkel?"

"Yes, I am," he replied.

And the old witch shouted in a rage, "Ah! Beware how you come again, for next time you shall not escape me!"

But Pinkel only laughed and rowed on.

The king was so delighted with the goat that he always kept it by his side, night and day, and, as he had promised, Pinkel was made ruler over the third part of the kingdom. As may be supposed, the brothers were more furious than ever.

"How can we get rid of him?" said one to the other. And at last they remembered the golden cloak.

"He will need to be clever if he is to take that!" they cried. And when next the king came to see his horses, they began to speak of Pinkel's cleverness—how he had managed to get the lantern and the goat, which nobody else would have been able to do.

"But as he was there, it is a pity he could not have brought away the golden cloak," they added.

"The golden cloak! What is that?" asked the king.

And the young men described its beauties in such glowing words that the king declared he would never know a day's happiness till he had wrapped the cloak round his own shoulders.

"And," he added, "the man who brings it to me shall wed my daughter and shall inherit my throne."

"None can get it but Pinkel," they said. For they did not imagine that the witch, after two warnings, could allow their brother to escape a third time. So Pinkel was sent for, and with a glad heart he set out.

He passed many hours inventing first one plan and then another, till he had a scheme ready which he thought might prove successful.

Thrusting a large bag inside his coat, he pushed off from the shore, taking care this time to reach the island in daylight. Having made his boat fast to a tree, he walked up to the hut, hanging his head and pretending to be both sorrowful and ashamed.

"Is that you, Pinkel?" asked the witch when she saw him, her eyes gleaming savagely.

"Yes, it is I," answered Pinkel.

"So you have dared, after all you have done, to put yourself in my power!" cried she. "Well, you shan't escape me this time!" And she took down a large knife and began to sharpen it.

"Oh, spare me!" shrieked Pinkel, falling on his knees and looking wildly about him.

"Spare you, indeed! Where are my lantern and my goat? No! No! There is only one fate for you!" And she held the knife in the air so that it glittered in the firelight.

"Then, if I must die," said Pinkel who, by this time, was *really* frightened, "let me at least choose my death. I am very hungry, for I have had nothing to eat all day. Put some poison, if you like, into the porridge, but at least let me have a good meal before I die."

"That is not a bad idea," answered the witch. And ladling out a large bowl of porridge, she stirred some poisonous herbs into it, and set about some work that had to be done. Then Pinkel hastily poured all the contents of the bowl into his bag, and made a great noise with his spoon, pretending that he was scraping up the last morsel.

"The porridge is excellent. Do give me some more," said Pinkel, turning toward her.

"Well, you have a fine appetite, young man," answered the witch. "However, it is the last time you will ever eat it, so I will give you another bowlful." And stirring in some herbs, she poured him out half of what remained, and then went to the window to call her cat.

In an instant Pinkel again emptied the porridge into the bag, and the next minute he rolled on the floor, twisting about and uttering loud groans. Suddenly he grew silent and lay still.

"Ah! I *thought* a second dose would be too much for you!" said the witch, looking at him. "I warned you what would happen if you came back. But why does not my lazy girl bring the wood I sent her for? It will soon be too dark for her to find her way. I suppose I must go and search for her. What a trouble girls are!"

The witch went to the door to watch if there were any signs of her daughter. But nothing could be seen of her, and heavy rain was falling.

"It is no night for my cloak," she muttered. "It would be covered with mud by the time I got back." So she took it off her shoulders and hung it up carefully. After that she put on her clogs and started to look for her daughter. As soon as the sound of the clogs had ceased, Pinkel jumped up, took down the cloak, and rowed off as fast as he could.

He had not gone far when a puff of wind unfolded the cloak, and its brightness shed light across the water. The witch, who was just entering the forest, turned round at that moment and saw the golden rays. She forgot all about her daughter, and ran down to the shore, screaming with rage at being outwitted a third time.

"Is that you, Pinkel?" she cried.

"Yes, it is I."

"Have you taken my golden cloak?"

"Yes, I have."

"Are you not a great knave?"

"Yes, truly, I am."

And so indeed he was!

But, all the same, he carried the cloak to the king's palace, and in return he received the hand of the king's daughter in marriage. People said that it was the bride who ought to have worn the cloak at her wedding feast, but the king was so pleased with it that he would not part from it, and to the end of his life was never seen without it.

After his death, Pinkel became king and gave up his bad ways and ruled his subjects well. As for his brothers, he did not punish them, but left them in the stables, where they grumbled all day long.

THE PUMPKIN GIANT

By MARY E. WILKINS

A VERY long time ago, there were no pumpkins. People had never eaten a pumpkin pie, or even stewed pumpkin—and that was the time when the Pumpkin Giant flourished.

There have been a great many giants who have flourished since the world began, and although a select few of them have been good giants, the majority of them have been so bad that their crimes even more than their size have gone to make them notorious. But the Pumpkin Giant was an uncommonly bad one, and his general appearance and behavior were such as to make one shudder to an extent that you would hardly believe possible. The convulsive shivering caused by the mere mention of his name, and, in some cases where the people were unusually sensitive, by the mere thought of him, was known as "the Giant's Shakes."

The Pumpkin Giant was very tall. He probably would have overtopped most of the giants you have ever heard of. I don't suppose the Giant who lived on the Beanstalk whom Jack visited, was anything to compare with him—nor that it would have been a possible thing for the Pumpkin Giant, had he received an invitation to spend an afternoon with the Beanstalk Giant, to accept, on account of his inability to enter the Beanstalk Giant's door, no matter how much he stooped.

The Pumpkin Giant had a very large yellow head, which was also smooth and shiny. His eyes were big and round, and glowed like coals of fire. You would almost have thought that his head was lit up inside with candles. Indeed there was a rumor to that effect among the common people, but that was all nonsense, of course. No one of the more enlightened class credited it for an instant. His mouth, which stretched half around his head, was furnished with rows of pointed teeth, and he was never known to hold it any other way than wide open.

The Pumpkin Giant lived in a castle, as a matter of course. It is not fashionable for a giant to live in any other kind of a dwelling —why, nothing would be more tame and uninteresting than a giant in a two-story white house with green blinds and a picket fence, or even a brownstone front, if he could get into either of them, which he could not.

The Giant's castle was situated on a mountain, as it ought to have been, and there was also the usual courtyard before it, and the customary moat, which was full of— bones! All I have got to say about these bones is, they were not mutton bones.

The Pumpkin Giant was fonder of little boys and girls than anything else in the world—but he was somewhat fonder of little boys, and more particularly of *fat* little boys.

The fear and horror of this Giant extended over the whole country. Even the King on his throne was so severely afflicted with the Giant's Shakes that he had been obliged to have the throne propped, for fear it would topple over in some unusually violent fit. There was good reason why the King shook: his only daughter, the Princess Ariadne Diana, was probably the fattest princess in the whole world at that date. So fat was she that she had never walked a step in the dozen years of her life, being totally unable to progress over the earth by any method except rolling. And a really beautiful sight it was, too, to see the Princess Ariadne Diana, in her cloth-of-gold rolling-suit, faced with green velvet and edged with ermine, with her glittering crown on her head, trundling along the avenues of the royal gardens, which had been furnished with strips of rich carpeting for her express accommodation.

But gratifying as it would have been to the King, her sire, under other circumstances, to have had such an unusually interesting daughter, it now only served to fill his heart with the greatest anxiety on her account. The Princess was never allowed to leave the palace without a bodyguard of fifty knights, the very flower of the King's troops, with lances in rest, but in spite of all this precaution, the King shook.

Meanwhile, among the ordinary people

who could not procure an escort of fifty armed knights for the plump among their children, the ravages of the Pumpkin Giant were frightful. It was even feared at one time that there would be very few fat little girls, and no fat little boys at all, left in the kingdom. And what made matters worse, at that time the Giant commenced taking a tonic to increase his appetite.

Finally the King, in desperation, issued a proclamation that he would knight anyone, be he noble or common, who would cut off the head of the Pumpkin Giant. This was the King's usual method of rewarding any noble deed in his kingdom. It was a cheap method, and besides, everybody liked to be a knight.

When the King issued his proclamation, every man in the kingdom who was not already a knight, immediately tried to contrive ways and means to kill the Pumpkin Giant. But there was one obstacle which seemed insurmountable: they were afraid, and all of them had the Giant's Shakes so badly that they could not possibly have held a knife steady enough to cut off the Giant's head, even if they had dared to go near enough for that purpose.

There was one man who lived not far from the terrible Giant's castle, a poor man, his only worldly wealth consisting of a large potato field and a cottage in front of it. But he had a boy of twelve, an only son, who rivaled the Princess Ariadne Diana in point of fatness. He was unable to have a bodyguard for his son, so the amount of terror which the inhabitants of that humble cottage suffered day and night was heart-rending. The poor mother had been unable to leave her bed for two years, on account of the Giant's Shakes. Her husband barely got a living from the potato field. Half the time he and his wife had hardly enough to eat, as it naturally took the larger part of the potatoes to satisfy the fat little boy, their son. Their situation was truly pitiable.

The fat boy's name was Aeneas, his father's name was Patroclus, and his mother's Daphne. It was all the fashion in those days to have classical names. And as that was a fashion as easily adopted by the poor as the rich, everybody had them. They were just like Jim and Tommy and May in these days. Why, the Princess's name, Ariadne Diana, was nothing more or less than Ann Eliza with us.

One morning Patroclus and Aeneas were out in the field digging potatoes, for new potatoes were just in the market. The Early Rose potato had not been discovered in those days; but there was another potato, perhaps equally good, which attained to a similar degree of celebrity. It was called the Young Plantagenet, and reached a very large size indeed, much larger than the Early Rose does in our time.

Well, Patroclus and Aeneas had just dug perhaps a bushel of Young Plantagenet potatoes. It was slow work with them, for Patroclus had the Giant's Shakes badly that morning, and of course Aeneas was not very swift. He rolled about among the potato hills after the manner of the Princess Ariadne Diana—but he did not present as imposing an appearance as she, in his homespun farmer's frock.

All at once the earth trembled violently. Patroclus and Aeneas looked up and saw the Pumpkin Giant coming with his mouth wide open. "Get behind me, oh, my darling son!" cried Patroclus.

Aeneas obeyed, but it was of no use; for you could see his cheeks on each side of his father's waistcoat.

Patroclus was not ordinarily a brave man, but he was brave in an emergency— and as that is the only time when there is the slightest need of bravery, it was just as well.

The Pumpkin Giant strode along faster and faster, opening his mouth wider and wider, until they could fairly hear it crack at the corners.

Then Patroclus picked up an enormous Young Plantagenet and threw it plump into the Pumpkin Giant's mouth. The Giant choked and gasped, and choked and gasped, and finally tumbled down and died.

Patroclus and Aeneas, while the Giant was choking, had run to the house and locked themselves in. Then they looked out of the kitchen window. When they saw the Giant tumble down and lie quite still, they knew he must be dead. Then Daphne was immediately cured of the Giant's Shakes, and got out of bed for the first time in two years. Patroclus sharpened the carving knife on the kitchen stove, and they all went out into the potato field.

They cautiously approached the prostrate Giant, for fear he might suddenly spring up at them and—Aeneas. But no, he did not move at all. He was quite dead. And, all taking turns, they hacked off his head with the carving knife. Then Aeneas had it to play with, which was quite appropriate, and a good instance of the sarcasm of destiny.

The King was notified of the death of the Pumpkin Giant, and was greatly rejoiced thereby. His Giant's Shakes ceased, the props were removed from the throne, and the Princess Ariadne Diana was allowed to go out without her bodyguard of fifty knights, much to her delight, for she found them a great hindrance to the enjoyment of her daily outings. It was a great cross, not to say an embarrassment, when she was gleefully rolling in pursuit of a charming red and gold butterfly, to find herself suddenly stopped short by an armed knight with his lance at rest.

But the King, though his gratitude for the

noble deed knew no bounds, omitted to give the promised reward and knight Patroclus.

I hardly know how it happened—I don't think it was anything intentional. Patroclus felt rather hurt about it, and Daphne would have liked to be a lady, but Aeneas did not care in the least. He had the Giant's head to play with and that was reward enough for him. There was not a boy in the neighborhood but envied him his possession of such a unique plaything—and when they would stand looking over the wall of the potato field with longing eyes, and he was flying over the ground with the head, his happiness knew no bounds. Aeneas played so much with the Giant's head that finally late in the fall it got broken and scattered all over the field.

Next spring all over Patroclus's potato field grew running vines, and in the fall Giant's heads. There they were, all over the field—hundreds of them! Then there was consternation, indeed! The natural conclusion to be arrived at when the people saw the yellow Giant's heads making their appearance above the ground was that the rest of the Giants were coming.

"There was one Pumpkin Giant before," said they. "Now there will be a whole army of them! If it was dreadful then, what will it be in the future? If one Pumpkin Giant gave us the Shakes so badly, what will a whole army of them do?"

But when some time had elapsed and nothing more of the Giants appeared above the surface of the potato field, and as, moreover, the heads had not yet displayed any sign of opening their mouths, the people began to feel a little easier, and the general excitement subsided somewhat, although the King had ordered out Ariadne's bodyguard again.

Now Aeneas had been born with a propensity for putting everything into his mouth and tasting it. There was scarcely anything in his vicinity which could by any possibility be tasted, which he had not eaten a bit of. This propensity was so alarming in his babyhood that Daphne purchased a book of antidotes. And if it had not been for her admirable good judgment in doing so, this story would probably never have been told; for no human baby could possibly have survived the heterogeneous diet which Aeneas had indulged in. There was scarcely one of the antidotes which had not been resorted to from time to time.

Aeneas had become acquainted with the peculiar flavor of almost everything in his immediate vicinity except the Giant's heads; and he naturally enough cast longing eyes at them. Night and day he wondered what a Giant's head could taste like, till finally one day when Patroclus was away he stole out into the potato field, cut a bit out of one of the Giant's heads, and ate it. He was almost afraid to, but he reflected that his mother could give him an antidote; so he ventured. It tasted very sweet and nice. He liked it so much that he cut off another piece and ate that, then another and another, until he had eaten two-thirds of a Giant's head. Then he thought it was about time for him to go in and tell his mother and take an antidote, though he did not feel ill at all yet.

"Mother," said he, rolling slowly into the cottage, "I have eaten two-thirds of a Giant's head, and I guess you had better give me an antidote."

"Oh, my precious son!" groaned Daphne. "How could you?" She looked in her book of antidotes, but could not find one antidote for a Giant's head.

"Oh, Aeneas, my dear, dear son!" cried Daphne. "There is no antidote for Giant's head! What shall we do?"

Then she sat down and wept, and Aeneas wept, too, as loud as he possibly could. And he apparently had excellent reason to, for it did not seem possible that a boy could eat two-thirds of a Giant's head and survive it without an antidote. Patroclus came home, and they told him, and he sat down and lamented with them. All day they sat weeping and watching Aeneas, expecting every moment to see him die. But he did not die. On

the contrary, he had never felt so well in his
life.

Finally at sunset Aeneas looked up and
laughed. "I am not going to die," said he. "I
never felt so well. You had better stop crying.
And I am going out to get some more of that
Giant's head. I am hungry."

"Don't, don't!" cried his father and mother.

But he went, for he generally took his own way, very like most only sons. He came back with a whole Giant's head in his arms.

"See here, Father and Mother," cried he. "We'll all have some of this. It evidently is not poison, and it is good—a great deal better than potatoes!"

Patroclus and Daphne hesitated, but they were hungry, too. Since the crop of Giant's heads had sprung up in their field instead of potatoes, they had been hungry most of the time; so they tasted.

"It is good," said Daphne, "but I think it would be better cooked." So she put some in a kettle of water over the fire and let it boil awhile. Then she dished it up, and they all ate it. It was delicious. It tasted more like stewed pumpkin than anything else. In fact, it *was* stewed pumpkin.

Daphne was inventive, and something of a genius, and next day she concocted another dish out of the Giant's heads. She boiled them, and sifted them, and mixed them with eggs and sugar and milk and spice. Then she lined some plates with puff paste, filled them with the mixture, and set them in the oven to bake.

The result was unparalleled. Nothing half so exquisite had ever been tasted. They were all in ecstasies, Aeneas in particular. They gathered all the Giant's heads and stored them in the cellar. Daphne baked pies of them every day, and nothing could surpass the happiness of the whole family.

One morning the King had been out hunting, and happened to ride by the cottage of Patroclus with a train of his knights. Daphne was baking pies as usual, and the kitchen door and window were both open, for the room was too warm, so the delicious odor of the pies perfumed the whole air about the cottage.

"What is it smells so utterly lovely?" exclaimed the King, sniffing in a rapture.

He sent his page in to see.

"The housewife is baking Giant's-head pies," said the page, returning.

"What?" thundered the King. "Bring out one to me!"

So the page brought out a pie to him, and after all his knights had tasted to be sure it was not poison, and the King had watched them sharply for a few moments to be sure they were not killed, he tasted, too.

Then he beamed. It was a new sensation, and a new sensation is a great boon to a king.

"I never tasted anything so altogether superfine, so utterly magnificent, in my life!" cried the King. "Stewed peacock's tongues from the Baltic are not to be compared with it! Call out the housewife immediately!"

So Daphne came out trembling, and Patroclus and Aeneas, also.

"What a charming lad!" exclaimed the King as his glance fell upon Aeneas. "Now tell me about these wonderful pies, and I will reward you as becomes a monarch!"

Then Patroclus fell on his knees and related the whole history of the Giant's-head pies from the beginning.

The King actually blushed. "And I forgot to knight you, oh, noble and brave man, and to make a lady of your admirable wife!"

Then the King leaned gracefully down from his saddle and struck Patroclus with his jeweled sword and knighted him on the spot.

The whole family went to live at the royal palace. The roses in the royal garden were uprooted, and Giant's heads (or pumpkins, as they came to be called) were sown in their stead. All the royal parks also were turned into pumpkin fields.

Patroclus was in constant attendance on the King, and used to stand all day in his antechamber. Daphne had a position of great responsibility, for she superintended the baking of the pumpkin pies, and Aeneas finally married the Princess Ariadne Diana.

They were wedded in great state by fifty archbishops, and all the newspapers united in stating that they were the most charming and well-matched young couple that had ever been united in the kingdom.

The stone entrance of the Pumpkin Giant's castle was securely fastened, and upon it was engraved an inscription composed by the first poet in the kingdom, for which the King made him laureate, and gave him the liberal pension of fifty pumpkin pies per year.

The following is the inscription in full:

Here dwelt the Pumpkin Giant once,
He's dead the nation doth rejoice,
For, while he was alive, he lived
By e—g dear, fat, little boys.

The inscription is said to remain to this day. If you were to go there, you would probably see it.

THE DRAGON OF THE NORTH

VERY long ago there lived a terrible monster who came out of the North and laid waste to the countryside, devouring both men and animals. And this monster was so destructive that it was feared that unless help came, no living creature would be left on earth. Nothing could hurt it, because its whole body was covered with scales which were harder than stone or metal. Its two great eyes shone by night, and even by day, like the brightest lamps, and anyone who had the ill luck to look into those eyes became bewitched and rushed of his own accord into the monster's jaws.

In this way the dragon was able to feed upon both men and beasts without the least trouble to itself, as it did not have to move from the spot where it was lying. All the neighboring kings had offered rich rewards to anyone who would be able to destroy the monster, either by force or enchantment. Many had tried their luck, and all had failed. Once a great forest in which the dragon lay had been set on fire. The forest was burned down, but the fire did not do the monster the least harm.

However, it was said among the wise men that the dragon might be overcome by one who possessed King Solomon's signet ring, upon which a secret writing was engraved. This inscription would enable anyone wise enough to interpret it to find out how the dragon could be destroyed. But no one knew where the ring was hidden, nor was there any sorcerer or learned man to be found who would be able to explain the inscription.

At last a young man of courage set out to search for the ring. He went toward the sunrising, because he knew that all the wisdom of old times came from the East. After some years he met a famous Eastern magician and asked for his advice in the matter. The magician answered:

"Men can give you no help, but the birds of the air would be better guides to you, if you could learn their language. I can help you to understand it if you will stay with me a few days."

The youth thankfully accepted the magician's offer and said: "I cannot offer you any reward for your kindness, but if I succeeded, your trouble would be richly repaid."

Then the magician brewed a powerful potion out of nine herbs which he had gathered by moonlight, and gave the youth nine spoonfuls of it daily for three days, which made him able to understand the language of birds.

At parting, the magician said to him: "If you ever find Solomon's ring, bring it to me, so that I may explain the inscription on the ring to you, for there is no one else in the world who can do this."

From then on, the young man never felt lonely as he walked along. He always had company, because he understood the language of birds. In this way he learned many things which human knowledge could never have taught him. But time went on and he heard nothing about the ring.

One evening, when he was hot and tired, he sat down under a tree in a forest to eat his supper, and saw two birds sitting at the top of the tree. They were talking about him. The first bird said:

"That wanderer under the tree has come far in search of King Solomon's lost ring."

The old bird answered: "He will have to seek help from the witch-maiden. If she has not got the ring herself, she knows well enough who has it."

"But where is he going to find the witch-maiden?" said the first bird. "She is here today and gone tomorrow. He might as well try to catch the wind."

The other replied: "I do not know where she is at present, but in three nights she will come to the spring to wash her face, as she does every month when the moon is full, in order that she may never grow old nor wrinkled."

"Well," said the first bird, "the spring is not far from here. Shall we go and see how she does it?"

"Willingly, if you like," said the other.

The youth immediately decided to follow the birds to the spring. Only two things made him uneasy—first, that he might be asleep when the birds went, and secondly, that he might lose sight of them, since he had no wings to carry him along swiftly. He was too tired to keep awake all night, yet his anxiety prevented him from sleeping soundly, and when with the earliest dawn he looked up to the treetop, he was glad to see the birds still asleep with their heads under their wings. He ate his breakfast and waited, but the birds did not leave the place all day. They hopped about from one tree to another looking for food until evening, when they went back to sleep.

The next day the same thing happened, but on the third morning one bird said to the other: "Today we must go to the spring to see the witch-maiden wash her face." They remained on the tree till noon. Then they flew away and went toward the south.

The young man's heart beat with anxiety, afraid that he might lose sight of his guides, but he managed to keep the birds in view until they again settled upon a tree. The young man ran after them until he was quite out of breath, and after three short rests the birds at last reached a small open space in the forest. When the youth had overtaken them, he saw that there was a clear spring in the middle of the space. He sat down at the foot of the tree upon which the birds were perched, and listened to what they were saying to each other.

"The sun is not down yet," said the first bird. "We must wait till the moon rises and the maiden comes to the spring. Do you think she will see that young man?"

"Nothing is likely to escape her eyes, certainly not a young man," said the other bird.

"We will wait," said the first bird, "and see how they get on together."

The full moon was already shining down upon the forest when the young man heard a slight rustling sound. After a few moments a maiden came out of the forest, gliding over the grass so lightly that her feet seemed scarcely to touch the ground, and stood beside the spring. The youth had never in his life seen a woman so beautiful.

Without seeming to notice anything, the maiden went to the spring, looked up to the full moon, and knelt down and bathed her face nine times. Then she looked up to the moon again and walked nine times round the well, and sang this song:

"Full-faced moon with light unshaded,
Let my beauty ne'er be faded.
Never let my cheek grow pale!
While the moon is waning nightly,
May the maiden bloom more brightly,
May her freshness never fail!"

Then she dried her face with her long hair and was about to go away, when she turned toward the tree. The young man rose and stood waiting. Then the maiden said:

"You ought to be punished because you have watched my secret doings in the moonlight. But I will forgive you this time, because you are a stranger and knew no better. But you must tell me truly who you are and how you came to this place."

The youth answered humbly: "Forgive me, beautiful maiden, if I have unintentionally offended you. I chanced to come here after long wandering, and found a good place to sleep under this tree. At your coming I did not know what to do, but stayed where I was." And then he told her of his search for the ring.

The maiden said: "No man is able entirely to understand the power of this ring, because no one thoroughly understands the secret signs engraved upon it. But even with my half-knowledge, I can work great wonders. If I put the ring upon the little finger of my left hand, I can fly through the air wherever I wish to go. If I put it on the third finger of my left hand, I am invisible, and I can see everything that passes around me, though no one can see me. If I put the ring upon the middle finger of my left hand, neither fire nor water nor any sharp weapon can hurt me. If I put it on the forefinger of my left hand, I can with its help build houses or anything I desire. Finally, as long as I wear the ring on the thumb of my left hand, that hand is so strong that it can break rocks and walls. Besides these, the ring has other secrets of great importance."

When the youth heard all this, he said: "I do not think it possible that the ring can have all the power you say it has."

Then the maiden opened a box and took the ring out. It glittered like the clearest sunbeam. She put it on the middle finger of her left hand and told the youth to take a knife and try as hard as he could to cut her with it, for he would not be able to hurt her. He was unwilling at first, but the maiden insisted, so he tried to strike her with the knife, but an invisible wall seemed to be between them, and the maiden stood before him laughing and unhurt. Then she put the ring on her third finger and in an instant she had vanished from his eyes. Presently she was beside him again, laughing and holding the ring between her fingers.

"Do let me try to see if I can do these wonderful things," said the youth.

The maiden, suspecting no trickery, gave him the magic ring.

The young man pretended to have forgotten what to do, and asked what finger he must put the ring on so that no sharp weapon could hurt him.

"Oh, the middle finger of your left hand," the maiden answered, laughing.

She took the knife and tried to strike him, and he even tried to cut himself with it, but found it impossible. Then he asked the maiden to show him how to split stones and rocks with the help of the ring. So she led him to a great boulder.

"Now," she said, "put the ring upon the thumb of your left hand, and you will see how strong that hand has become." The youth did so, and found to his astonishment that with a single blow of his fist the stone flew into a thousand pieces.

Then the youth reckoned that this was a chance which, once lost, might never return. So while they stood laughing at the shattered stone, he placed the ring, as if in play, upon the third finger of his left hand.

"Now," said the maiden, "you are invisible to me until you take the ring off again."

But the youth had no mind to do that. On the contrary, he went farther off, then put the ring on the little finger of his left hand and soared into the air like a bird.

When the maiden saw him flying away, she thought at first that he was still playing and cried: "Come back, for now you see I have told you the truth." But the young man never came back.

Then the maiden saw she was deceived,

and bitterly repented that she had ever trusted him with the ring.

The young man never halted in his flight until he reached the house of the wise magician who had taught him the speech of birds. The magician was delighted to find that his search had been successful, and at once began to interpret the secret signs engraved upon the ring, but it took him seven weeks to make them out clearly. Then he gave the following instructions to overcome the dragon of the North:

"You must have an iron horse cast, which must have little wheels under each foot. You must also be armed with a spear two fathoms long, which you will be able to wield by means of the magic ring upon your left thumb. The spear must be as thick in the middle as a large tree, and both its ends must be sharp. In the middle of the spear you must have two strong chains ten fathoms in length. As soon as the dragon has made himself fast to the spear, which you must thrust through his jaws, you must spring quickly from the iron horse and fasten the ends of the chains firmly to the ground with iron stakes, so that he cannot get away from them. After two or three days, the monster's strength will be so exhausted that you will be able to approach him. Then you can put Solomon's ring upon your left thumb and give him the finishing stroke, but keep the ring on your third finger until you have come close to him, so that the monster cannot see you, else he might strike you dead with his long tail. But when all is done, take care you do not lose the ring and that no one takes it from you."

The young man thanked the magician for his directions and promised, should they succeed, to reward him. But the magician answered: "I have profited so much by the wisdom the ring has taught me that I desire no other reward."

Then they parted, and the youth quickly flew home through the air. After remaining in his own home for some weeks, he heard people say that the terrible dragon of the North was not far off and might shortly be expected in the country. The king announced publicly that he would give his daughter in marriage, as well as a large part of his kingdom, to any young man who would free the country from the monster.

The youth then went to the king and told him that he had good hopes of subduing the dragon if the king would grant him all he desired for that purpose. The king willingly agreed, and the iron horse, the great spear, and the chains were all prepared as the youth requested.

When all was ready, it was found that the iron horse was so heavy that a hundred men could not move it from the spot, so the youth found there was nothing for it but to move it with his own strength by means of the magic ring. The dragon was now so near that soon he would be over the frontier. The

youth now began to consider how to act, for
if he had to push the iron horse from behind
he could not ride upon it, as the sorcerer had
said he must.

A raven unexpectedly gave him this advice: "Ride upon the horse and push the spear against the ground, as if you were pushing off a boat from the land." The youth did so, and found that in this way he could easily move forward.

The dragon had his monstrous jaws wide open, all ready for his expected prey. A few paces nearer, and man and horse would have been swallowed up by them!

The youth trembled with horror and his blood ran cold, yet he did not lose his courage. Holding the iron spear upright in his hand, he brought it down with all his might right through the monster's lower jaw. Then he sprang from his horse before the dragon had time to shut his mouth. A fearful clap of thunder, which could be heard for miles around, now warned him that the dragon's jaws had closed upon the spear. When the youth turned round, he saw the point of the spear sticking up high above the dragon's upper jaw, and knew that the other end must be fastened firmly to the ground. But the dragon had got his teeth fixed in the iron horse, which was now useless. The youth now fastened down the chains by means of the enormous iron pegs which he had provided.

The death struggle of the monster lasted three days and three nights. In his writhing he beat his tail so violently that the earth trembled as during an earthquake. When he finally lost power to move his tail, the youth with the help of the ring took up a stone which twenty ordinary men could not have moved, and beat the dragon so hard about the head with it that very soon the monster lay lifeless before him.

Great was the rejoicing when the news was spread that the terrible monster was dead. His conqueror was received into the city with as much pomp as if he had been the mightiest of kings.

The old king did not need to urge his daughter to marry the slayer of the dragon. He found her already willing to bestow her hand upon this hero, who had done what whole armies had tried in vain to do. A magnificent wedding was celebrated, at which the rejoicings lasted four whole weeks, for all the neighboring kings had met together to thank the man who had freed the world from their common enemy.

NIX·NAUGHT·NOTHING

ONCE upon a time there lived a King and a Queen who had no children, and this made them very sad indeed. Now it so happened that the King had to go and fight battles in a far country, and he was away for many long months. And while he was away, the Queen at last bore him a little son. She was delighted, and thought how pleased the King would be when he came home and found that his dearest wish had been fulfilled. All the courtiers were pleased, too, and began to arrange a grand festival for the naming of the little Prince. But the Queen said, "No! The child shall have no name till his father gives it to him. Till then we will call him Nix-Naught-Nothing, because his father knows nothing about him!"

So little Prince Nix-Naught-Nothing grew into a strong, hearty lad—for his father did not come back for a long time, and did not even know that he had a son.

But at long last he turned homeward. On the way, he came to a big, rushing river, which neither he nor his army could cross, for the water was full of dangerous whirlpools.

So they were stopped, until a huge giant appeared who could take the river, whirlpool and all, in his stride. He said, "I'll carry you all over, if you like."

Now, though the giant smiled and was very polite, the King knew enough of giants to think it wiser to have a hard and fast bargain. So he said, "What's your pay?"

"Pay?" echoed the giant with a grin. "What do you take me for? Give me Nix-Naught-Nothing, and I'll do the job with a glad heart."

Now the King felt just a trifle ashamed at the giant's generosity, so he said, "Certainly, I'll give you nix-naught-nothing, and my thanks as well."

So the giant carried them safely over the stream and past the whirlpools, and the King hastened home. His dear wife, the Queen, showed him his young son, tall and strong for his age.

"And what's your name?" he asked of the child clasped in his arms.

"Nix-Naught-Nothing," answered the boy. "That's what they call me till my father gives me a name."

Well, the King nearly dropped the child, he was so horrified! "What have I done?" he cried. "I promised to give nix-naught-nothing to the giant who carried us over the whirlpools!"

At this the Queen wept and wailed. But being a clever woman, she thought of a plan to save her son. She said to her husband the King, "If the giant comes to claim his promise, we will give him the hen-wife's youngest boy. She has so many, she will not mind if we give her some money, and the giant will never know the difference."

Sure enough, the very next morning the
giant appeared to claim Nix-Naught-Nothing, and they dressed up the hen-wife's boy
in the Prince's clothes and cried when the
giant carried off his prize. But after a while
he came to a big stone, sat down to rest, and
fell asleep. When he awoke, he started up
and called out:

76

*"Hodge, Hodge, on my shoulders! Say
What d'ye make the time o' day?"*

And the hen-wife's little boy replied:

*"Time that my mother the hen-wife takes
The eggs for the wise Queen's breakfast
cakes!"*

Then the giant saw at once the trick that
had been played on him, and he threw the
hen-wife's boy on the ground, so that his
head hit on the stone and he was killed.

Then the giant strode back to the palace
and demanded Nix-Naught-Nothing. This
time they dressed up the gardener's boy, and
wept when the giant carried his prize off on
his back. Then the same thing happened.
The giant grew weary of his burden, sat
down on the big stone to rest, and fell asleep.
When he awoke, he called out:

*"Hodge, Hodge, on my shoulders! Say
What d'ye make the time o' day?"*

And the gardener's boy replied:

*"Time that my father the gardener took
Greens for the wise Queen's dinner to
cook!"*

The giant saw at once that a second trick had been played on him and became quite angry. He flung the boy from him so that he was killed, and then strode back to the palace, where he cried out, "Give me what you promised to give—Nix-Naught-Nothing—or I will destroy you all."

Then they saw they must give up the dear little Prince, and this time they really cried as the giant carried off the boy. And this time, after the giant had had his rest at the big stone, and had awakened and called:

"Hodge, Hodge, on my shoulders! Say
What d'ye make the time o' day?"

the little Prince replied:

"Time for the King my father to call
'Let supper be served in the banquet-
ing hall.' "

Then the giant laughed with glee and rubbed his hands saying, "I've got the right one at last." He took Nix-Naught-Nothing to his own house under the whirlpools, for the giant was really a great Magician who could take any form he chose. And the reason he wanted a little prince so badly was that he had lost his wife, and had only one little daughter who needed a playmate.

Nix-Naught-Nothing and the Magician's daughter grew up together and every year made them fonder of each other, until she promised to marry him.

Now the Magician had no idea that his daughter would marry just an ordinary human prince, so he looked for some way in which he could quietly get rid of Nix-Naught-Nothing. One day he said, "I have work for you, Nix-Naught-Nothing. There is a stable nearby which is seven miles long and seven miles wide, and it has not been cleaned for seven years. By tomorrow evening you must have cleaned it, or I will have you for my supper."

Well, before dawn, Nix-Naught-Nothing set to work at his task, but as fast as he cleared the muck, it just fell back again, so by breakfast-time he was no nearer the end of the job than at the start.

The Magician's daughter, coming to bring him his breakfast, found him so distraught that he could hardly speak to her.

"We'll soon set that to rights," she said. So she just clapped her hands and called:

"Beasts and birds o' each degree,
Clean me this stable for love o' me."

And in a minute the beasts of the fields came trooping, and the sky was dark with the wings of birds. They carried away the muck, and the stable was as clean as a new pin before evening.

Now when the Magician saw this, he grew angry, and he guessed it was his daughter's magic that had brought about the miracle. So he said: "Shame on the wit that helped you! But I have a harder job for you tomorrow. Yonder is a lake seven miles long, seven miles broad, and seven miles deep. Drain it by nightfall, so that not one drop remains, or I shall eat you for supper."

So once again Nix-Naught-Nothing rose before dawn, and began his task. But though he baled out water without ceasing, it always ran back, so that by breakfast-time he was no nearer the end of his job.

When the Magician's daughter came with his breakfast, she only laughed and said, "I'll soon fix that!" Then she clapped her hands and called:

"Oh! all ye fish of river and sea,
Drink me this water for love of me!"

And lo and behold! the lake was thick with fishes. They drank and drank, till not one drop remained.

Now when the Magician returned in the

morning and saw this, he was as angry as could be. He knew it was his daughter's magic, so he said: "Double shame on the wit that helped you. Yet it betters you not, for I will give you a harder task than the last. If you do that, you may have my daughter. Over there is a tree seven miles high, and no branch to it till the top, where there is a nest with some eggs in it. Bring those eggs down without breaking one, or, sure as fate, I'll eat you for my supper."

Then the Magician's daughter was very sad, for with all her magic she could think of no way of helping her lover to fetch the eggs and bring them down unbroken. So she sat with Nix-Naught-Nothing under the tree, and thought and thought, until an idea came to her, and she clapped her hands and cried:

"Fingers of mine, for love of me,
Help my true lover to climb the tree."

Then her fingers dropped off her hands one by one and arranged themselves like the steps of a ladder up the tree. But there were not quite enough of them to reach the top, so she cried again:

"Oh, toes of mine, for love o' me,
Help my true lover to climb the tree."

Then her toes began to drop off one by one and arrange themselves like the rungs of a ladder. But when the toes of one foot had gone to their places, the ladder was tall enough. So Nix-Naught-Nothing climbed up it, reached the nest and got the seven eggs.

As he was coming down with the eggs, he was so overjoyed at having finished his task that he turned to see if the Magician's daughter was happy, too. And the seventh egg slipped from his hand and broke.

"Quick! Quick!" cried the Magician's daughter. "There is nothing to do now but to leave at once. But first I must have my magic flask, or I shall be unable to help. It is in my room and the door is locked. Put your fingers, since I have none, in my pocket, take the key, unlock the door, get the flask, and follow me fast. I shall go slower than you, for I have no toes on one foot!"

So Nix-Naught-Nothing did as she asked, and soon caught up to the Magician's daughter. But alas! they could not run fast, so before long the Magician, who had once again taken a giant's form in order to have a long stride, could be seen behind them. Nearer and nearer he came, until he was just going to seize Nix-Naught-Nothing, when the Magician's daughter cried: "Put your fingers, since I have none, into my hair, take my comb and throw it down."

So Nix-Naught-Nothing did as she asked, and lo and behold! out of every one of the

comb-prongs there sprang up a prickly briar, which grew so fast that the Magician found himself in the middle of a thorn hedge! Nix-Naught-Nothing and his sweetheart had time for a good start, but the Magician's daughter could not run fast because she had lost her toes on one foot. Therefore, the Magician in giant form soon caught up again, and he was just about to grasp Nix-Naught-Nothing when the Magician's daughter cried: "Put your fingers, since I have none, to my breast. Take out my veil-dagger and throw it down."

So he did as she asked, and in a moment the dagger had grown to thousands of sharp razors, criss-cross on the ground, and the Magician giant was howling with pain as he trod among them.

Nix-Naught-Nothing and his sweetheart were nearly out of sight before the giant could start again. Yet it wasn't long before he caught up. For the Magician's daughter could not run fast, because she had lost her toes on one foot! She did what she could, but it was no use. Just as the giant was reaching out a hand to lay hold of Nix-Naught-Nothing, she cried, breathlessly:

"There's nothing left but the magic flask. Take it out and sprinkle some of what it holds on the ground."

And Nix-Naught-Nothing did as she asked. But in his hurry he nearly emptied the flask altogether. And so the big, big wave of water which instantly welled up, swept him off his feet, and would have carried him away, had not the Magician's daughter's loosened veil caught him and held him fast. But the wave grew behind them, until it reached the giant's waist. Then it grew and grew until it reached his shoulders. And it

grew and grew until it swept over his head—
a great big sea-wave full of little fishes and
crabs and sea-snails and all sort of strange
creatures.

So that was the last of the Magician giant.
But the Magician's daughter was so weary
that, after a time, she couldn't move another
step, and she said to her lover, "Yonder are
lights burning. Go and see if you can find a
night's lodging. I will climb this tree by the
pool where I shall be safe, and by the time
you return I shall be rested."

Now, it happened by chance that the
lights they saw were the lights of the castle
where Nix-Naught-Nothing's father and
mother, the King and Queen, lived (though,
of course, he did not know this). As he walked
toward the castle, he came upon the hen-
wife's cottage and asked for a night's lodging.

"Who are you?" asked the hen-wife suspi-
ciously.

"I am Nix-Naught-Nothing," replied the
young man.

Now the hen-wife still grieved over her
boy who had been killed, so she instantly re-
solved to be revenged.

"I cannot give you a night's lodging," she

said. "But you shall have a drink of milk, for you look tired. Then you can go on to the castle and beg for a bed there."

So she gave him a cup of milk. But, being a witch-woman, she put a potion to it so that at the very moment he saw his father and mother he would fall fast asleep, and no one would be able to waken him.

Now the King and Queen had never ceased grieving for their lost son, so they were always very kind to wandering young men, and when they heard that one was begging a night's lodging, they went down to the hall to see him. And lo! the moment Nix-Naught-Nothing caught sight of his father and mother, there he was on the floor fast asleep, and none could waken him! And he did not recognize his father and mother and they did not recognize him.

But Prince Nix-Naught-Nothing had grown into a very handsome young man, so they pitied him, and when no one could waken him, the King said, "A maiden will likely take more trouble to waken him than others, seeing how handsome he is, so send forth a proclamation that if any maiden in my realm can waken this young man, she shall have him in marriage, and a handsome dowry as well."

So the proclamation was sent forth, and all the pretty maidens of the realm came to try their luck, but they had no success.

Now the gardener whose boy had been killed by the giant had a daughter who was very ugly indeed—so ugly that she thought it no use to try her luck, and went about her work as usual. So she took her pitcher to the pool to fill it. Now the Magician's daughter was still hiding in the tree, waiting for her lover to return. Thus it came to pass that the gardener's ugly daughter, bending down to fill her pitcher in the pool, saw a beautiful reflection in the water, and thought that it was her own!

"If I am as pretty as that," she cried, "I'll draw water no longer!"

So she threw down her pitcher, and went straight to the castle to see if she hadn't a chance to get the handsome stranger and the handsome dowry. But of course she hadn't— though at the sight of Nix-Naught-Nothing she fell so much in love with him that, knowing the hen-wife to be a witch, she went to her and offered all her savings for a charm by which she could awaken the sleeper.

Now when the hen-wife witch heard her tale, she thought it would be a rare revenge to marry the King and Queen's long-lost son to a gardener's ugly daughter, so she promptly took the girl's savings and gave her a charm by which she could unspell the Prince or spell him again at her pleasure.

So away went the gardener's daughter to
the castle, and sure enough, no sooner had
she sung her charm, than Nix-Naught-Nothing awoke.

"I am going to marry you," she said coax-
ingly—but Nix-Naught-Nothing said he
would prefer sleep. She thought it wiser to
put him to sleep again till the marriage feast
was ready, and she had got her fine clothes,
so she spelled him asleep again.

Now the gardener had, of course, to draw the water himself, since his daughter would not work. He took the pitcher to the pool. And he also saw the Magician's daughter's reflection in the water, but he did not think the face was his own, since *he* had a beard!

Then he looked up and saw the lady in the tree.

She, poor thing, was half-dead with sorrow, hunger and fatigue, so, being a kind man, he took her to his house and gave her food. And he told her that that *very day* his daughter was to marry a handsome young stranger at the castle, and would get a handsome dowry from the King and Queen, in memory of their son, Nix-Naught-Nothing, who had been carried off by a giant when he was a little boy.

Then the Magician's daughter felt sure that something had happened to her lover, so she went to the castle, and there she found him fast asleep in a chair.

But she could not waken him, for her magic had gone from her with the magic flask which Nix-Naught-Nothing had emptied.

So, though she put her fingerless hands on his and wept, he never stirred nor woke.

Now one of the old servants there, seeing how she cried, took pity on her and said, "She that is to marry the young man will be back before long and unspell him for the wedding. Hide yourself and listen to her charm."

So the Magician's daughter hid herself, and by-and-by the gardener's daughter came along in her fine wedding-dress, and began to sing her charm. But the Magician's daughter didn't wait for her to finish it, for the moment Nix-Naught-Nothing opened his eyes, she rushed out of her hiding place and put her fingerless hands in his.

Then Nix-Naught-Nothing remembered everything. He remembered the castle, he remembered his father and mother, he remembered the Magician's daughter and all that she had done for him.

Then he drew out the magic flask and said, "Surely, surely there must be enough magic in it to mend your hands." And there was. There were just fourteen drops left, ten for the fingers and four for the toes. But there was not one for the little toe, so it could not be brought back.

Of course, after that there was great rejoicing, and Prince Nix-Naught-Nothing and the Magician's daughter were married and lived happily ever after, even though she only had four toes on one foot.

As for the hen-wife witch, she was not heard from again, and so the gardener's daughter got back her earnings. But she was not happy, because her shadow in the water was ugly again.

THE GIANT WHO HAD
NO HEART IN HIS BODY

ONCE upon a time there was a King who had seven sons, and he loved them so much that one of them always had to be with him. Now, when they were grown up, six were to set off to find brides. As for the youngest, his father kept him at home, and the others were to bring back a Princess for him to the palace.

The King gave the six the finest clothes, and each had his horse. And so they set off.

When they had been to many palaces, and seen many Princesses, they came at last to a King who had six daughters. Such lovely King's daughters they had never seen, and so they courted them, and when they had got them for sweethearts, they set off home again, but they quite forgot that they were to bring back with them a sweetheart for Boots, their brother.

But when they had traveled a while, they passed close by a steep hillside, like a wall, where the Giant's house was, and there the Giant came out, set his eyes upon them, and turned them all into stone, Princes and Princesses and all.

The King waited and waited for his six sons, but the more he waited, the longer they stayed away. He said he would never know what it was to be glad again.

"And if I had not you left," he said to Boots, "I would live no longer, so full of sorrow am I for the loss of your brothers."

"Well, but now I've been thinking to ask your leave to set out and find them again. That's what I'm thinking of," said Boots.

"No," said his father. "You shall never leave, for then you would stay away, too."

But Boots had set his heart upon it; and he begged so long that the King was forced to let him go. The King had no other horse to give Boots but an old broken-down nag, but Boots did not mind. He sprang up on his sorry old steed.

"Farewell, Father," said he. "I'll come back, never fear, and I shall bring my six brothers back with me." With that he rode off.

When he had ridden a while, he came to a Raven, which lay in the road and flapped its wings, and was not able to get out of the way, it was so starved.

"Oh, dear friend," said the Raven, "give me a little food, and I'll help you again at your utmost need."

"I haven't much food," said the Prince, "and I don't see how you'll ever be able to help me much. Still, I can spare you a little. I see you want it."

So he gave the Raven some of the food he had brought with him.

Now, when he had gone a bit farther, he came to a brook, and near it lay a Salmon, which had got upon a dry place and dashed itself about, and could not get into the water again.

"Oh, dear friend," said the Salmon to the Prince, "put me into the water again, and I'll help you again at your utmost need."

"Well," said the Prince, "the help you'll give me will not be great, I dare say, but it's a pity you should lie there." And with that he tossed the fish into the stream.

After that he went a long way, and met a Wolf, which was so famished that it lay and crawled along the road on its belly.

"Dear friend, do let me have your horse," said the Wolf. "I'm so hungry, the wind whistles through my ribs. I've had nothing to eat these two years."

"No," said Boots, "this will never do. First I came to a Raven, and I was forced to give him my food. Next I came to a Salmon, and I had to help him into the water again. And now you want my horse. It can't be done, that it can't, for then I will have nothing to ride on."

"But you can help me," said Graylegs the Wolf. "You can ride upon my back, and I'll help you again in your utmost need."

"Well, the help I shall get from you will not be great, I'll bet," said the Prince, "but you may take my horse, since you are in such need."

So when the Wolf had eaten the horse, Boots took the bit and put it into the wolf's jaw, and laid the saddle on his back. And now the Wolf was so strong, after what he had got inside, that he set off with the Prince like the wind.

"When we have gone a bit farther," said Graylegs, "I'll show you the Giant's house."

So after a while they came to it.

"See, here is the Giant's house," said the Wolf. "And see, here are your six brothers, whom the Giant has turned into stone. And see, here are their six brides. And yonder is the door, and in at that door you must go."

"But I dare not go in," said the Prince. "He'll take my life."

"No, no!" said the Wolf. "When you get in, you'll find a Princess, and she'll tell you what to do to make an end of the Giant. Only do just as she bids you."

Boots went in, but, truth to say, he was very much afraid. When he came in, the Giant was away, but in one of the rooms sat the Princess, just as the Wolf had said, and a lovely Princess she was, too.

"Oh, heaven help you! Why have you come?" said the Princess, as she saw him. "It will surely be your death. No one can ever destroy the Giant who lives here, for he has no heart in his body."

"Well, well!" said Boots. "But now that I am here, I may as well see what I can do with him. And I will see if I can't free my brothers, who are standing turned to stone outside. And you, too, I will try to save— that I will."

"Well, if you must, you must," said the Princess. "And so let us see if we can't hit on a plan. Just creep under the bed yonder, and listen to what he and I talk about. But please, do lie as still as a mouse."

So he crawled under the bed, and he had just got underneath it, when the Giant arrived.

After a while, the Princess said:

"There is one thing I'd like to ask you about, if only I dared."

"What is that?" asked the Giant.

"Tell me where it is you keep your heart, since you don't carry it about you," said the Princess.

"Ah, that's a thing you've no business to ask about. But if you must know, it lies under the door-sill," said the Giant.

"Ho, ho!" said Boots to himself under the bed. "Then we'll soon see if we can't find it."

Next morning the Giant got up and strode off to the wood, but he was hardly out of the house before Boots and the Princess set to work to look under the door-sill for his heart. But the more they dug, and the more they hunted, the more they couldn't find it.

"He has fooled us this time," said the Princess, "but we'll try him once more."

So she picked all the prettiest flowers she could find and spread them over the door-sill which they had replaced. When the time came for the Giant to come home again,

Boots crawled under the bed. Just as he was well under, back came the Giant.

A little while later, he asked who had strewn flowers about the door-sill.

"Oh, I, of course," said the Princess.

"And what's the meaning of all this?" said the Giant.

"Ah!" said the Princess. "I'm so fond of you that I couldn't help strewing them, when I knew that your heart lay under there."

"You don't say so!" said the Giant. "But it really doesn't lie there at all."

So the Princess asked the Giant again where his heart was, for she said she would like to know.

"Well," said the Giant, "if you must know, it lies in the cupboard against the wall."

"So, so!" thought Boots and the Princess. "Then we'll soon try to find it."

Next morning the Giant was away early, and strode off to the wood, and so soon as he was gone, Boots and the Princess were hunting for his heart. But the more they sought for it, the less they found it.

"Well," said the Princess, "we'll just try him once more."

So she decked out the cupboard with flowers and garlands, and when the time came for the Giant to come home, Boots crawled under the bed again.

Then back came the Giant.

A little while after, the Giant saw the cupboard decked about with flowers and garlands, so he asked who had done that. Who could it be but the Princess?

"And what's the meaning of all this tomfoolery?" asked the Giant.

"Oh, I'm so fond of you, I couldn't help doing it when I knew that your heart lay there," said the Princess.

"How can you be so silly as to believe any such thing?" said the Giant. "Where my heart is, you will never come."

"Well," said the Princess, "but for all that, 'twould be such a pleasure to know where it really lies."

Then the Giant could hold out no longer, but was forced to say:

"Far, far away in a lake lies an island. On that island stands a church. In that church is a well. In that well swims a duck. In that duck there is an egg. And in that egg there lies my heart."

In the morning early, while it was still gray dawn, the Giant strode off to the wood.

"Yes, now I must set off, too," said Boots. "If I only knew how to find the way."

He took a long, long farewell of the Princess, and when he got out of the Giant's door, there stood the Wolf waiting for him. So Boots told him all that had happened inside the house, and said now he wished to ride to the well in the church, if he only knew the way.

The Wolf told him to jump on his back—
he'd soon find the way. And away they went,
over hedge and field, over hill and dale.

After they had traveled many, many days,
they came at last to the lake. Then the
Prince did not know how to get over it, but
the Wolf told him not to be afraid, but stick
on. And so he jumped into the lake with the
Prince on his back, and swam over to the island. So they came to the church. But the
church keys hung high, high up on the top of
the tower, and at first the Prince did not
know how to get them down.

"You must call on the Raven," said the
Wolf.

So the Prince called on the Raven, and immediately the Raven came, and flew up and
fetched the keys, and so the Prince got into
the church.

But when he came to the well, there was
the duck, just as the Giant had said. So the
Prince stood and coaxed it and coaxed it, till
it came to him, and he grasped it in his hand.
But just as he lifted it up from the water,
the duck dropped the egg into the well, and
then Boots was beside himself to know how
to get it out again.

"Well, now you must call on the Salmon, to be sure," said the Wolf. And the King's son called on the Salmon, and the Salmon came and fetched up the egg from the bottom of the well.

Then the Wolf told him to squeeze the egg, and as soon as he squeezed it, the Giant screamed out.

"Squeeze it again," said the Wolf. And the Giant screamed still more piteously.

"Tell him that if he will restore to life again your six brothers and their brides, whom he has turned to stone, you will spare his life," said the Wolf. Yes, the Giant was ready to do that, and he turned the six brothers into King's sons again, and their brides into King's daughters.

"Now, squeeze the egg in two," said the Wolf. So Boots squeezed the egg to pieces, and the Giant burst at once.

Now, when he had made an end of the Giant, Boots rode back again on the Wolf to the Giant's house, and there stood all his six brothers alive and merry, with their brides. Then Boots went into the hillside after *his* bride, and so they all returned home to their father's house.

THE WITCH

ONCE upon a time there was a peasant whose wife died, leaving him with two children—twins—a boy and a girl. For some years the poor man lived on alone with the children, caring for them as best he could. But everything in the house seemed to go wrong without a woman to look after it, and at last he made up his mind to marry again, feeling that a wife would bring peace and order to his household and take care of his motherless children.

So he married, but peace and order did not come to the household. The stepmother was very cruel to the twins, and beat them, and half-starved them, and constantly drove them out of the house. Her one idea was to get them out of the way. All day she thought of nothing but how to get rid of them, and at last an evil idea came into her head. She arranged to send them out into the great gloomy wood where a wicked witch lived. One morning she spoke to them, saying:

"You have been such good children that I am going to send you to visit my granny, who lives in a dear little hut in the wood. You will have to wait upon her and serve her, but you will be well rewarded, for she will give you the best of everything."

So the children left the house together, and the little sister, who was very wise for her years, said to the brother:

"We will first go and see our own dear grandmother and tell her where our stepmother is sending us."

110

And when the grandmother had heard where they were going, she cried and said:

"You poor children! How I pity you! And yet I can do nothing to help you! Your stepmother is not sending you to her granny, but to a wicked witch. Now listen to me, children. You must be civil and kind to everyone, and never say a cross word to anyone and never touch a crumb belonging to anyone else. Who knows if, after all, help may not be sent to you?"

And she gave her grandchildren a bottle of milk, and a piece of ham and a loaf of bread, and they set out for the great gloomy wood. When they reached it, they saw in front of them, in the thickest of the trees, a queer little hut, and when they looked into it, there lay the witch, with her head on the threshold of the door, with one foot in one corner and the other in the other corner, and her knees cocked up, almost touching the ceiling.

"Who's there?" she snarled in an awful voice when she saw the children.

And they answered civilly, though they were so terrified that they hid behind one another, and said:

"Good morning, granny. Our stepmother

has sent us to wait upon you and serve you."

"See that you do it well, then," growled the witch. "If I am pleased with you, I'll reward you. But if I am not, I'll put you in a pan and fry you in the oven—that's what I'll do with you!"

So saying, she set the girl down to spin yarn and gave the boy a sieve in which to carry water from the well, and she herself went out into the wood.

Now, as the girl was sitting at her distaff, weeping bitterly because she could not spin, she heard the sound of hundreds of little feet, and from every hole and corner in the hut mice came pattering along the floor, squeaking and saying:

"Little girl, why are your eyes so red?
If you want help, then give us some
bread."

And the girl gave them the bread that her grandmother had given her. Then the mice told her that the witch had a cat, and the cat was very fond of ham. If she would give the cat her ham, it would show her the way out of the wood, and in the meantime they would spin the yarn for her.

So the girl set out to look for the cat, and as she was hunting about, she met her brother, in great trouble because he could not carry water from the well in a sieve, as it came pouring out as fast as he put it in. And as she was trying to comfort him, they heard a rustling of wings, and a flight of wrens alighted on the ground beside them. And the wrens said:

"Give us some crumbs, then you need not grieve,
For you'll find that water will stay in a sieve."

Then the twins crumbled their bread on the ground, and the wrens pecked it and chirruped and chirped. And when they had eaten the last crumb, they told the boy to fill up the holes of the sieve with clay and then to draw water from the well. So he did what they said, and carried the sieve full of water into the hut without spilling a drop.

When they entered the hut, the cat was curled up on the floor. So they stroked her, and fed her with ham, and said to her:

"Pussy, gray pussy, tell us how we are to get away from the witch."

Then the cat thanked them for the ham and gave them a handkerchief and a comb, and told them that when the witch pursued them, as she certainly would, all they had to do was to throw the handkerchief on the ground and run as fast as they could. As soon as the handkerchief touched the ground, a deep, broad river would spring up, which would hinder the witch's progress. If she managed to get across it, they must throw the comb behind them and run, for where the comb fell a dense forest would spring up, which would delay the witch so long that they would be able to get safely away.

The cat had scarcely finished speaking when the witch returned to see if the children had fulfilled their tasks.

"Well, you have done well enough for to-day," she grumbled, "but tomorrow you'll have something more difficult to do, and if you don't do it well, you pampered brats, straight into the oven you go."

Frightened and trembling in every limb, the poor children lay down to sleep on a heap of straw in the corner of the hut. But they dared not close their eyes and scarcely ventured to breathe. In the morning the witch gave the girl two pieces of linen to weave before night and the boy a pile of wood to cut into chips. Then the witch left them to their tasks and went out into the wood.

As soon as the witch was out of sight, the children took the comb and the handkerchief, and taking one another by the hand, they ran, and ran, and ran. And first they met the watchdog, who was going to leap on them and tear them to pieces. But they threw the remainder of their bread to him, and he ate and wagged his tail. Then they were hindered by the birch trees, whose branches almost put their eyes out. But the little sister tied the twigs together with a piece of ribbon and they got past safely, and after running through the wood came out upon the open fields.

In the meantime, in the hut, the cat was busy weaving the linen and tangling the threads as it wove. The witch returned to see how the children were getting on, and she crept up to the window and whispered:

"Are you weaving, my little dear?"

"Yes, Granny, I am weaving," answered the cat.

When the witch saw that the children had escaped her, she was furious, and said: "Why did you let the children leave the hut? Why did you not scratch their eyes out?"

But the cat curled up its tail and put its back up and answered: "I have served you all these years, and you never even threw me a bone, but the dear children gave me their own piece of ham."

Then the witch was furious with the watchdog and with the birch tree because they had let the children pass. But the dog answered:

"I have served you all these years and you never gave me so much as a hard crust, but the dear children gave me their own loaf of bread."

And the birch rustled its leaves and said: "I have served you longer than I can say, and you never even tied a bit of twine round my branches. The dear children bound them up with their brightest ribbons."

So the witch saw there was no help to be got from her old servants, and that the best thing she could do was to mount her broom and set off in pursuit of the children. As the children ran, they heard the sound of the broom sweeping the ground close behind them, so instantly they threw the handkerchief down over their shoulder, and in a moment a deep, broad river flowed behind them.

When the witch came up to it, it took her a long time before she found a place where she could ford over on her broomstick—but at last she got across and continued the chase faster than before. And as the children ran, they heard a sound, and the little sister put her ear to the ground and heard the broom sweeping the earth close behind them. So, quick as thought, she threw the comb down on the ground, and in an instant, as the cat had said, a dense forest sprang up,

in which the roots and branches were so
closely intertwined that it was impossible to
force a way through it. So when the witch
came up to it on her broom, she found there
was nothing to do but to turn round and go
back to her hut.

But the twins ran straight on till they
reached their own home. Then they told
their father all they had suffered, and he was
so angry with their stepmother that he drove
her out of the house and never let her return. But he and the children lived happily
together, and he took care of them himself
and never let a stranger come near them.

THE DRAGON AND HIS GRANDMOTHER

THERE was once a great war, and the King had a great many soldiers, but he gave them so little pay that they could not live upon it. Then three of them decided to leave.

One of them said to the others, "If we are caught, we shall be hanged on the gallows. How shall we arrange it?"

The other said, "Do you see that large cornfield there? If we were to hide ourselves in that, no one could find us. The army cannot come into it, and tomorrow it is to march on."

They crept into the corn, but the army did not march on. It remained encamped close around them. They sat for two days and two nights in the corn, and grew so hungry that they nearly died. But if they were to go out, it was certain death.

They said at last, "What use was it our deserting? We must perish here miserably."

While they were speaking, a fiery dragon came flying through the air. It hovered near them, and asked why they were hidden there.

They answered, "We are three soldiers, and have left the King's service because our pay was so small. Now if we remain here, we shall die of hunger, and if we move out, we shall die on the gallows."

"If you will serve me for seven years," said the dragon, "I will lead you through the army so that no one shall catch you."

"We have no choice, and must take your offer," said they.

Then the dragon seized them in his claws, took them through the air over the army, and set them down a long way from it.

He gave them a little whip, saying, "Whip and slash with this, and as much money as you want will jump up before you. You can live as great lords, keep horses, and drive about in carriages. But after seven years you are mine."

Then he put a book before them, which he made all three of them sign. "I will then give you a riddle," he said. "If you guess it, you shall be free and out of my power."

The dragon then flew away, and they moved on with their little whip. They had as much money as they wanted, wore fine clothes, and made their way into the world. Wherever they went, they lived in merry-making and splendor, drove about with horses and carriages, ate and drank, but did nothing wrong.

The time passed quickly away, and when the seven years were nearly ended, two of them grew terribly anxious and frightened, but the third made light of it, saying, "Don't be afraid, brothers, I wasn't born yesterday. I will guess the riddle."

They went into a field, sat down, and the
two had sad faces. An old woman passed by,
and asked them why they were so sad.

"What have you to do with it? You cannot
help us," they replied.

"Who knows?" she answered. "Tell me of
your trouble."

Then they told her that they had become the servants of the dragon for seven long years, and how he had given them money as plentifully as blackberries. But as they had signed their names, they were his, unless when the seven years had passed they could guess a riddle.

The old woman said, "If you would help yourselves, one of you must go into the wood, and there he will come upon a tumble-down building of rocks which looks like a little house. He must go in, and there he will find help."

The two melancholy ones thought, "That won't save us!" and they remained where they were. But the third and merry one jumped up and went into the wood till he found the rock hut. In the hut sat a very old woman, who was the dragon's grandmother. She asked him how he came, and what was his business there. He told her all that had happened, and because she was pleased with him, she said she would help him.

She lifted up a large stone which lay over the cellar, saying, "Hide yourself there. You can hear all that is spoken in this room. Only sit still and don't stir. When the dragon comes, I will ask him what the riddle is, for he tells me everything. Then listen carefully to what he answers."

At midnight the dragon flew in and asked for his supper. His grandmother set the table and brought out food and drink till he was satisfied, and they ate and drank together. Then in the course of the conversation she asked him what he had done during the day.

"I haven't had much luck today," he said, "but I have tight hold on three soldiers."

"Indeed! Three soldiers!" said she. "Who cannot escape you?"

"They are mine," answered the dragon scornfully, "for I have given them one riddle which they will never be able to guess."

"What sort of a riddle is it?" she asked.

"I will tell you this. In the North Sea lies a dead sea-cat—that shall be their roast meat. And the rib of a whale—that shall be their silver spoon. And the hollow foot of an old horse—that shall be their wineglass."

When the dragon had gone to bed, his old grandmother pulled up the stone and let out the soldier.

"Did you pay attention to everything?"

"Yes," he replied. "I know enough, and can help myself splendidly."

Then he went by another way through the window secretly, and in all haste back to his friends. He told them how the dragon had been outwitted by his grandmother, and how he had heard from his own lips the answer to the riddle.

Then they were delighted and in high spirits. They took out their whip and cracked so much money that it came jumping up from the ground.

When the seven years had quite gone, the dragon came with his book, and, pointing at the signatures, said:

"I will take you underground with me. You shall have a meal there. If you can tell me what you will get for your roast meat, you shall be free, and shall also keep the whip."

Then said the first soldier, "In the North Sea lies a dead sea-cat. That shall be the roast meat."

The dragon was much annoyed, and hummed and hawed a good deal, and asked the second, "But what shall be your spoon?"

"The rib of a whale shall be our silver spoon."

The dragon made a face and growled again three times, "Hum, hum, hum," and said to the third, "Do you know what your wineglass shall be?"

"An old horse's hollow hoof shall be our wineglass."

Then the dragon flew away with a loud shriek, and had no more power over them. But the three soldiers took the little whip, whipped as much money as they wanted, and lived happily to their lives' end.